# GRANDMA'S SOUP

*For Avi, Chavi, Menachem, Malki, Shuli, Zev, Rafi, Bubby Gussie and Zayde Jack,*
*who know that "Grandma's Soup" is really "Bubby's Soup."—N.K.*

Library of Congress Cataloging-in-Publication Data

Karkowsky, Nancy Faye.
    Grandma's soup / Nancy Karkowsky; illustrated by Shelly O. Haas. p.      cm.
    Summary: A young girl confronts her grandmother's growing confusion and
disability from Alzheimer's disease.
    ISBN 0-930494-98-9: — ISBN 0-930494-99-7 (pbk.)
    [1. Alzheimer's disease—Fiction. 2. Grandmothers—Fiction. 3. Jews—United
States—Fiction.]  I Haas, Shelly O., ill.
II. Title.
PZ7.K1388Gr   1989
[E]—dc19                                                            89-30875
                                                                        CIP
                                                                        AC

Published by KAR-BEN COPIES, INC., Rockville, MD 1-800-4-KARBEN
Printed in the United States of America

# GRANDMA'S SOUP

## NANCY KARKOWSKY

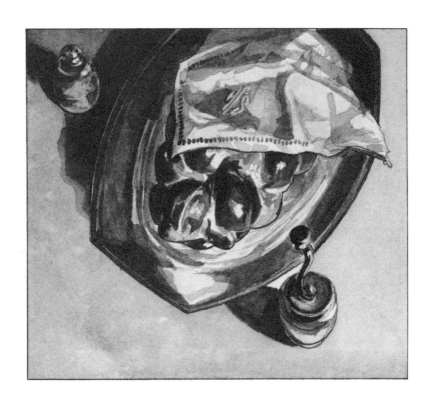

## ILLUSTRATIONS BY SHELLY O. HAAS

KAR-BEN COPIES INC.                    ROCKVILLE, MD

Whenever we went to my grandparents' house, we always had Grandma's soup.

Before each visit, my grandmother would say to my grandfather, "Jack, the children are coming for Shabbat. Go to the market and get me souping greens, and make sure they're fresh!"

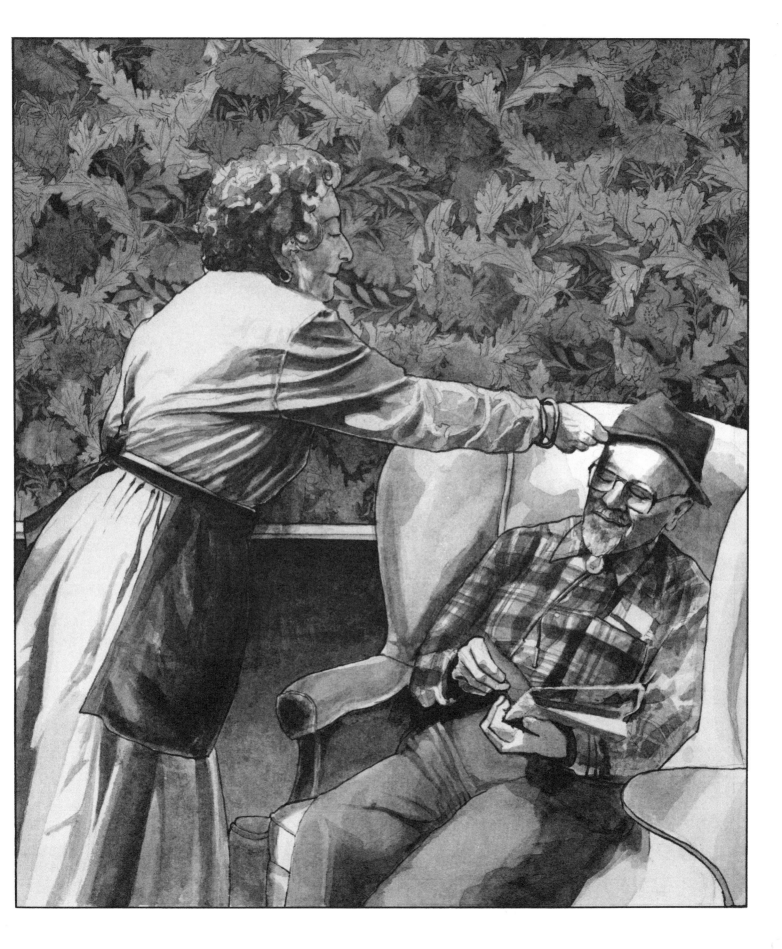

Then Grandpa would buy the sweetest carrots, the fattest onions, the leafiest celery, the whitest parsnip, the bushiest parsley, the chubbiest garlic, a bag of white lima beans, and a box of little yellow chickpeas, and bring them home to Grandma.

Grandma would peel the carrots, onions, parsnip, and garlic, and wash the celery, parsley, beans, and peas, and put them into a big pot with the pieces of chicken and the soup bones that she had prepared while Grandpa was shopping. She would add some salt, pepper, garlic powder, onion powder, paprika, two golden soup cubes from Israel, and lots of water. Then she would let it cook and cook and cook.

And we would eat and eat and eat. Sometimes I would finish two whole bowls, which would make Grandma happy.

"Such a big girl, such a nice girl," she would say.

Then one day the soup did not taste so good.

"Mom," my father said, "did you put something new in the soup?"

"Cloves," said my mother. "There are cloves in the soup."

Grandma looked upset.

"Cloves in the soup? Who would put cloves in soup? Cloves you put in spice cake or applesauce. Jack, did you put cloves in the soup?"

Grandpa shook his head.

"Tina," Grandma said firmly, "you don't know what you're talking about. I've been making this soup for 45 years. There are no cloves in it."

Nobody said anything, but only Grandma and Grandpa finished their soup.

The next time we went to my grandparents' house, the soup tasted okay.

"The soup tastes better this time," I said to my grandmother.

Grandma looked at me. "Who are you?" she asked.

I thought she was joking, but she didn't smile.

"I'm Eve," I told her.

"Eve?" Grandma said, as if she didn't know who I was.

"Yes, Mom," my mother said. "Eve. Abie's oldest daughter. You do know who Abie is?"

"Of course I know who Abie is," Grandma snapped.

Everyone looked relieved, but not for long.

"She looks a lot like a little girl I used to take care of," Grandma explained.

"I *am* the little girl you used to take care of, Grandma," I told her. My voice was shaking.

"Oh no, no, no," Grandma smiled at me as if I didn't know what I was talking about. "You're a big girl, much bigger than the one I took care of. She was a little girl, almost a baby." My mother squeezed my shoulders tightly.

"You're right, Mom," my mother said softly. "Eve is a big girl, much bigger than the one you used to take care of."

"Why didn't Grandma know who I was?" I asked my mother later.

"Grandma's not feeling well," my mother answered. "She's sick."

"She doesn't look sick," I said.

"She's not sick like that," my father said. He sounded angry and sad. "Sometimes when people get older, their minds play tricks on them. They get mixed up and don't remember things or people."

"Dr. Bachrach's old, and he remembers *everything*," my brother said.

"You're right," my father agreed. "Some people are lucky. Some people are not so lucky. But we still love them."

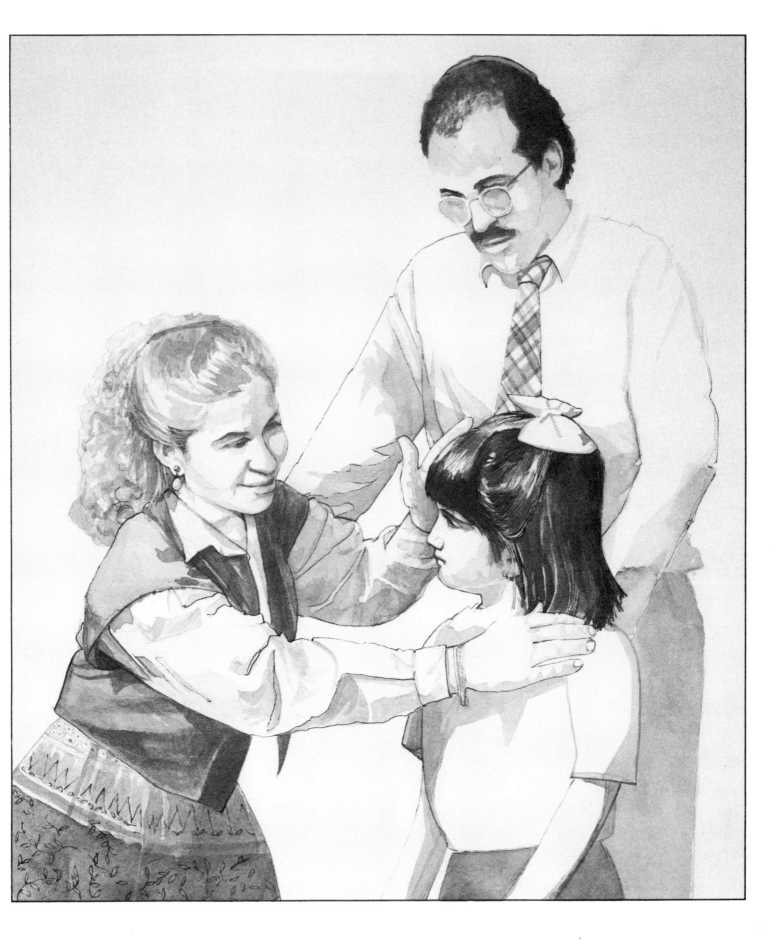

The next time we visited my grandparents, the soup had so much pepper in it, not even Grandma or Grandpa could eat it.

Grandma touched her head, and looked unhappily at Grandpa.

"What's happening to me, Jack? The soup is no good."

Grandpa looked like he was going to cry.

After dinner we put on our hats and coats and got ready to leave. Everyone kissed everyone else.

"Goodbye, goodbye," we said, "thank you for having us."
Grandma kissed my father.

"Thank you for coming," she told him. "But next time please bring your children."

"Mom, these are my children. These are your grandchildren," he said.

"Oh," said Grandma. "My memory isn't so good anymore."

Suddenly I began to cry. I couldn't help it. Tears came down my face faster and faster.

Grandma took me in her arms and her body was soft and warm and she held me tight. She hugged me and she whispered, "Don't cry my sweetheart, don't cry my precious, my big girl, my good girl, please don't cry." She hugged me some more.

I lifted my head and tried to smile.

"I'm okay, Grandma. I'm sorry I made your dress wet."

"Dresses aren't important. Children are important," she said. Then she turned to my parents. "You take care of this sweetheart here, she shouldn't get sick or anything."

She and Grandpa smiled and waved at us as we went down the hall.

As the door closed, I could hear Grandma saying, "When are the children going to visit us, Jack? I miss them so."

"Will Grandma get better soon?" I asked.

"No," said my mother. "I don't know if she'll ever get better. She may get worse."

"Worse?" said David. "Will we still have to visit her?"

"Yes," said my mother. "That is what families are for—to share the good times and the bad times. Sharing makes the good times happier and the bad times less sad."

So we still go to Grandma's house. Sometimes she knows who I am. Usually she doesn't. I hate it when she doesn't, but I don't cry anymore.

The soup is okay now. Grandpa makes it, though he still calls it "Grandma's Soup."

Sometimes I even have two bowls.